Hortense
and the
Shadow

*To our babička,
with love and plum cake*

Hachette Book Group supports the right to free expression and the value of copyright. The purpose of copyright is to encourage writers and artists to produce the creative works that enrich our culture.

The scanning, uploading, and distribution of this book without permission is a theft of the author's intellectual property. If you would like permission to use material from the book (other than for review purposes), please contact permissions@hbgusa.com. Thank you for your support of the author's rights.

Little, Brown and Company
Hachette Book Group
1290 Avenue of the Americas, New York, NY 10104
Visit us at LBYR.com

Originally published in 2017 by Puffin Books in Great Britain
First U.S. Edition: November 2017

Little, Brown and Company is a division of Hachette Book Group, Inc.
The Little, Brown name and logo are trademarks of Hachette Book Group, Inc.

The publisher is not responsible for websites (or their content) that are not owned by the publisher.

ISBNs: 978-0-316-44079-0 (hardcover), 978-0-316-44081-3 (ebook),
978-0-316-44084-4 (ebook), 978-0-316-44082-0 (ebook)

Printed in China

TLF

10 9 8 7 6 5 4 3 2 1

Hortense
and the
Shadow

Natalia and Lauren O'Hara

LITTLE, BROWN AND COMPANY
NEW YORK BOSTON

*T*hrough the dark
and wolfish woods,

through the white
and silent snow,

lived
a small girl
called
Hortense.

Though kind and brave,
she was sad as an owl because
of one thing.

Hortense

hated

her

shadow.

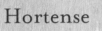

Everywhere she went,

it went.

Everything she did,

it did.

And every time night fell, it grew . . .
tall and dark
and crooked.

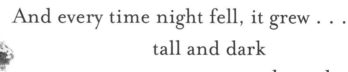

So Hortense started hiding
her shadow

behind
columns . . .

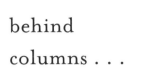

under sofas . . .

and in holes.

But every time she hid it,
her shadow grew

worse . . .

and worse . . .

and worse.

"I HATE you, shadow!"

yelled Hortense.

Then one bright morning
her shadow lay dark
on a step. . . .

As she fell,

Hortense knew

her shadow hated her too.

When evening came, Hortense crept out to the yard,
and then she dashed . . .

over the grass,

up the wall,

through the window,

and—as a raven cried
in a willow tree—

she slammed the sash down
and cut off her shadow!

The shadow howled and kicked,
and scratched the glass . . .

ran over the lawn,
and then at last . . .

was lost in the dusk.

Now the days are as bright as the first winter snow.

"Gone,

    gone,

        gone!" sings Hortense.

Only sometimes she feels like someone is watching,
quiet in the darkest corner.
"But the shadow is gone," she thinks.
"Now I am safe."

The night was black and full of strange sounds.
Wind flew through the woods like a pack of wild dogs.
Long after midnight, the door shook
with knocks.

Hortense woke with a jolt!
She slipped out of bed,
down the stairs,

through the hall,

out the door,
and then she saw . . .

nothing.

Just the dark.

But then her eyes grew used
to the dark and she saw . . .

one star . . .

torn clouds . . .

black trees

and . . .

BANDITS!

"Oh, bandits!" cried Hortense.
"There's nothing here! No jewels,
nor books, nor gold cuckoo clocks.
And the house is full of people!"

But, laughing and snorting
and shaking their fists,
the bandits came closer.

And as they crept in on every side . . .

something dark and terrible
flashed high above.

The bandits watched
with round, open mouths . . .

a hunter,

a baker, a farmer,

a bear!

And the bandits,
        stumbling,
            tumbled away.

The night was still. Snow fell on snow.
A lonely owl cried and
the bear turned away.

"Wait!" shouted Hortense.
She leapt up a tree, reached for the bear,
and touched . . .

her shadow.

"Oh, shadow," said Hortense. "I saw things all wrong.

"In the dark you were long to make me taller.
On prickly white days you shaded my eyes.
You stretched for miles to show how far I can go.

"What's a page without ink, or a deer without spots,
or a moon without night?
You're part of me, shadow.
Please come back!"

She reached for her shadow . . .
        and her shadow reached back.

They leapt
    and they crowed
        and they danced in the sun.

From that day to this day,
wherever she goes,
her shadow goes too.

And if it is sometimes dark, fierce,
strange, silly, jagged, or blue, well . . .

sometimes

Hortense is too.